THE
NIGHT-TIME
CAT and the
PLUMP GREY MOUSE
A TRINITY COLLEGE TALE

Erika McGann grew up in Drogheda, County Louth, and now lives in Dublin. She is the author of a number of children's books, including the winner of the Waverton Good Read Children's Prize 2014, *The Demon Notebook*, the first in her magical series about Grace and her four friends. Other books in the series are: *The Broken Spell*, *The Watching Wood* and *The Midnight Carnival*. She is also the author of the 'Cass and the Bubble Street Gang' series and the picture book *Where Are You, Puffling?*

Lauren O'Neill is an illustrator and graphic designer based in Dublin. Originally from Wexford, she moved to Dublin to study in NCAD and stayed. Her work has appeared in storybooks, advertising campaigns and gallery exhibitions. She has illustrated a retelling of Jonathan Swift's *Gulliver*, winning the Children's Books Ireland Honour Award for Illustration, and *Blazing a Trail*, Children's Book of the Year (Senior), Irish Book Awards 2018.

DEDICATIONS

For Cleo – EMcG

For Conor, our very own scholar – LO'N

ACKNOWLEDGEMENTS

Many thanks to Lauren for her glorious artwork, to Susan Houlden and Emma Byrne for making this book as wonderful as it could be, and to everyone at The O'Brien Press.

– EMcG

Thanks to Erika for her words and imagination, and to Susan and Emma, who made it all work together. – LO'N

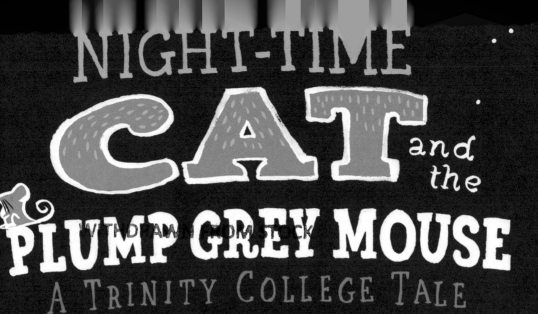

NIGHT-TIME
CAT and the
PLUMP GREY MOUSE

A TRINITY COLLEGE TALE

ERIKA McGANN

illustrated by
LAUREN O'NEILL

THE O'BRIEN PRESS
DUBLIN

First published 2019 by
The O'Brien Press Ltd,
12 Terenure Road East, Rathgar,
Dublin 6, Ireland.
Tel: +353 1 4923333; Fax: +353 1 4922777
E-mail: books@obrien.ie.
Website: www.obrien.ie
The O'Brien Press is a member of Publishing Ireland.

ISBN: 978-1-84717-945-6

8 7 6 5 4 3 2 1
23 22 21 20 19

Printed aand bound in Poland by Białostockie Zakłady Graficzne S.A.
The paper in this book is produced using pulp from managed forests.

The Night-time Cat and the Plump, Grey Mouse:
A Trinity College Tale
receives assistance from The Arts Council

Published in

DUBLIN

UNESCO
City of Literature

On a dark, dark night, in a very quiet library, there was an old, old, beautiful book. Looking out from the pages of the book was a plump, grey mouse. When the clock struck twelve, the little mouse blinked. He stretched his little legs and he hopped right off the page.

The mouse was not alone in the old, old
book. Four furry paws with very sharp claws
were creeping across the page.

'Mmm,' said Pangur Bán, the cat, 'I'm so
hungry. But where, oh where, did that plump,
grey mouse go?'

Pangur Bán walked through a long, long room, with lots of books and talking heads.

'Mr Swift,' said the cat to one of the talking heads, 'have you seen a little mouse? He's grey and plump and oh-so juicy.'

'You silly cat,' said the head of Jonathan Swift. 'You shouldn't eat that poor, poor mouse. Not even baked or boiled or stewed.'

But Pangur Bán was still hungry, and so she walked on alone.

Pangur Bán went looking for the mouse outside.

There in a dark, dark square with pretty trees and sparkling stars, a ghost sat on a windowsill.

'Mr Ford,' said Pangur Bán, 'have you seen a little mouse? He's grey and plump and oh-so yummy.'

'You silly cat,' the ghost replied. 'Students are not allowed out after dark. Neither are cats or mice. Get back to bed at once or I will fetch my pistol.'

But Pangur Bán was still hungry, and so she walked on alone.

H

Pangur Bán came to a field, where great big giants were chasing a ball. A king and queen were watching.

'Those little folk,' the king said, 'are no match for the giants.'

'Oh, just you watch,' the queen replied. 'They're faster than you think.'

Suddenly, the ball raced through the grass, like a fish caught
on a hook. Pangur Bán looked closer and saw tiny, tiny
people running underneath. They'd stolen the ball!
'Haha!' the queen cried. 'There they go! Those Lilliputians
have it now.'

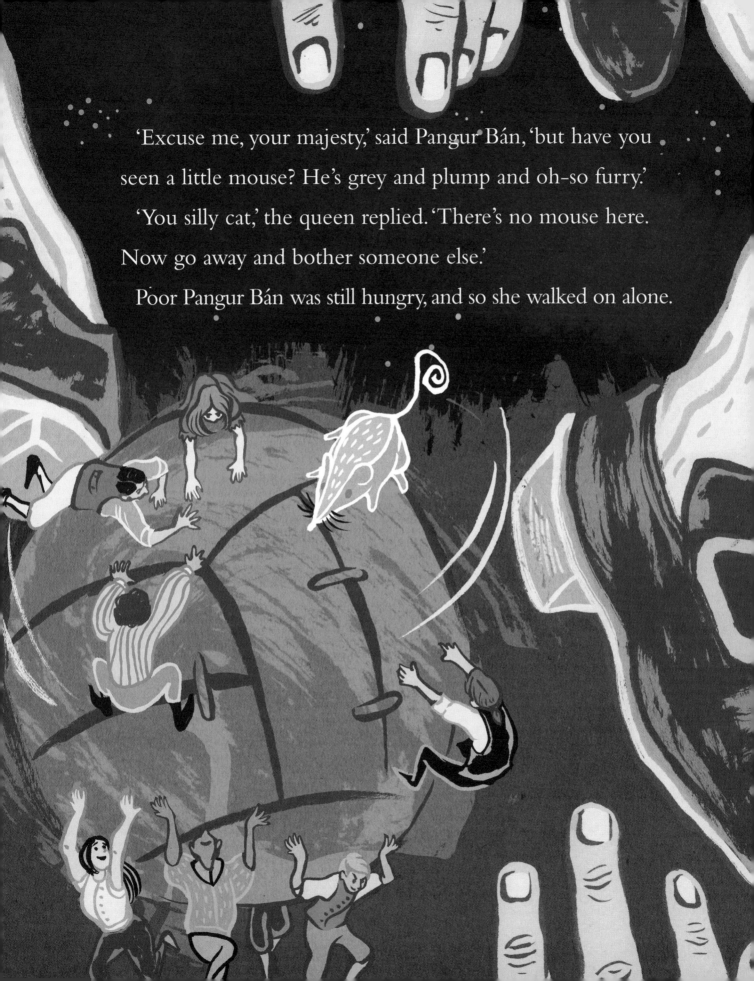

'Excuse me, your majesty,' said Pangur Bán, 'but have you seen a little mouse? He's grey and plump and oh-so furry.'

'You silly cat,' the queen replied. 'There's no mouse here. Now go away and bother someone else.'

Poor Pangur Bán was still hungry, and so she walked on alone.

Pangur Bán found a theatre, where all the actors were standing frozen on the stage.

The director saw the cat and shrieked, 'Places, everyone. Start the show! At once, at once! What are you waiting for? We've got an audience.'

'Mr Beckett,' said Pangur Bán, 'could you help me find a mouse? He's grey and plump and oh-so spicy.'

'You silly cat,' said the ghost of Samuel Beckett. 'We're putting this show on just for you. You'll have to stay and watch it now.'

But Pangur Bán was still hungry, and so she walked on alone.

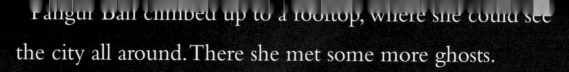

Pangur Bán climbed up to a rooftop, where she could see the city all around. There she met some more ghosts.

'We're supposed to be up there, with the stars,' one ghost said when she saw the cat, 'but we got stuck below. Would you like to be a star? You can have my parachute.'

'Oh no,' said the cat. 'I'm looking for a mouse. He's grey and plump and oh-so pudgy. Have you seen him?'

'You silly cat,' the ghost replied. 'A mouse would run along the ground. We're far too busy looking up. Why don't you join us in the sky?'

But Pangur Bán was still hungry, and so she walked on alone.

Pangur Bán walked through a secret door and found a cellar. Two ghosts were having a duel, but they were using books instead of swords.

'My stories are scarier than yours,' Sheridan Le Fanu said. 'They'd make a monster shriek.'

'Ha!' said Bram Stoker. 'Your stories wouldn't even scare my granny. My books are so frightening they'd make a werewolf cry.'

'Then meet my Carmilla!' Le Fanu shook his book and out popped his scary vampire.

'Say hello to Count Dracula!' Stoker flipped his book and out came his scary vampire.

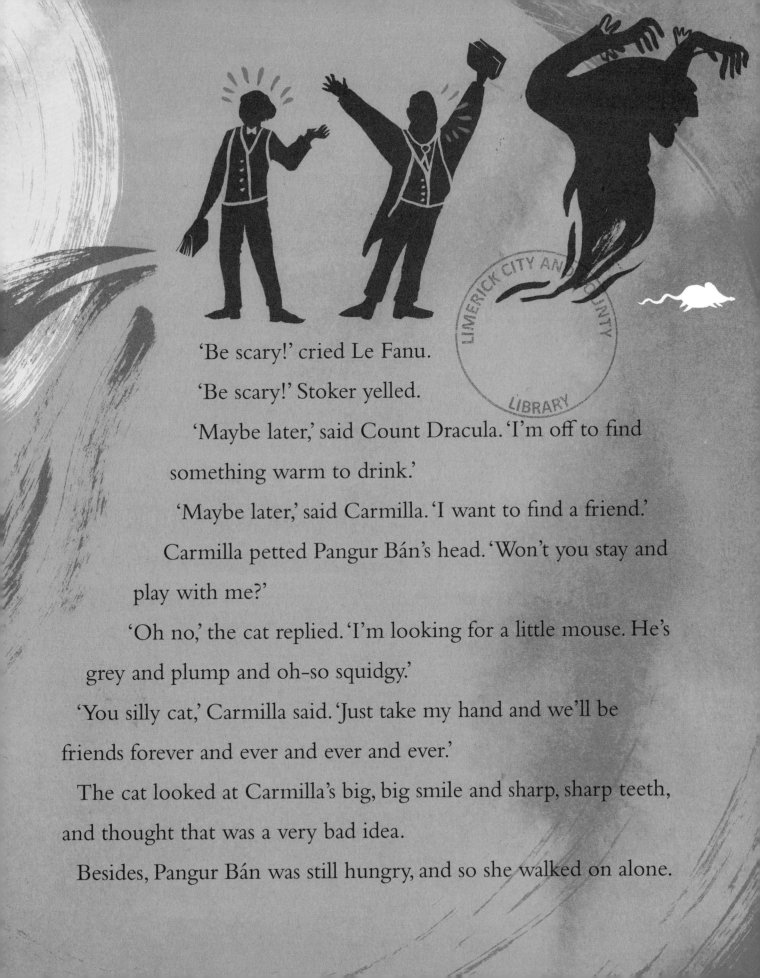

'Be scary!' cried Le Fanu.

'Be scary!' Stoker yelled.

'Maybe later,' said Count Dracula. 'I'm off to find something warm to drink.'

'Maybe later,' said Carmilla. 'I want to find a friend.'

Carmilla petted Pangur Bán's head. 'Won't you stay and play with me?'

'Oh no,' the cat replied. 'I'm looking for a little mouse. He's grey and plump and oh-so squidgy.'

'You silly cat,' Carmilla said. 'Just take my hand and we'll be friends forever and ever and ever and ever.'

The cat looked at Carmilla's big, big smile and sharp, sharp teeth, and thought that was a very bad idea.

Besides, Pangur Bán was still hungry, and so she walked on alone.

In a tall, tall library, the cat came across another ghost who was opening book after book after book after book. But he never sat down to read.

'Mr Marsh,' said Pangur Bán, 'could you help me find a mouse? He's grey and plump and oh-so meaty.'

'You silly cat,' the ghost replied. 'Can't you see I'm busy? I'm looking for a letter. It's a goodbye note from my niece, and it's hidden in a book somewhere. You must stay and help me find it.'

But Pangur Bán was still hungry, and so she walked on alone.

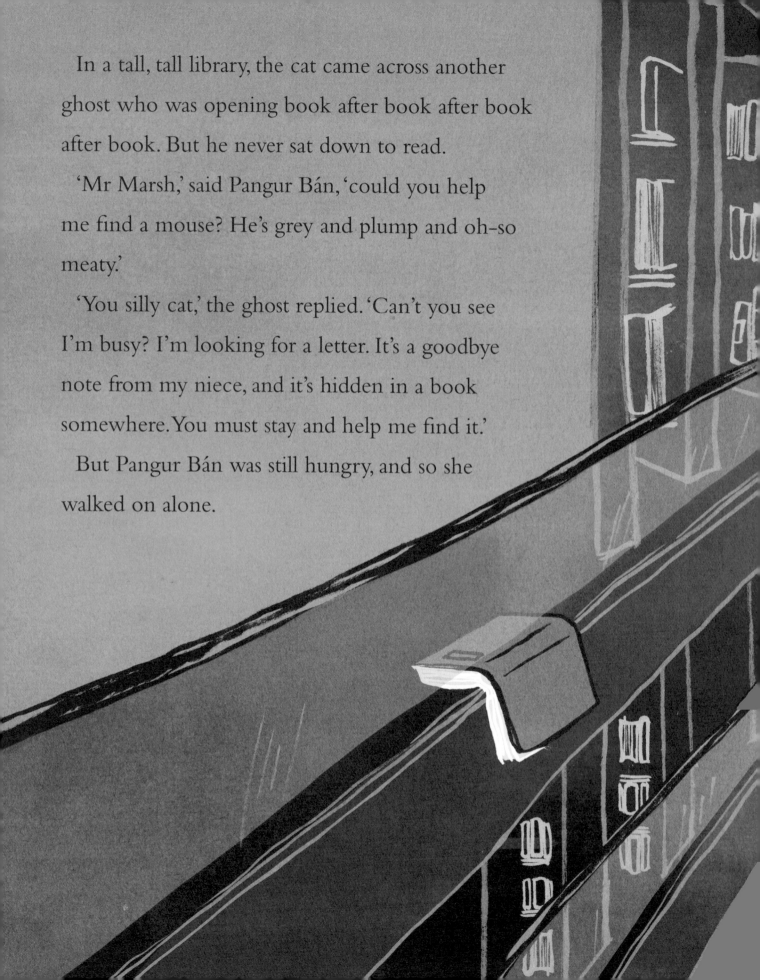

Pangur Bán found a swimming pool that bubbled and spat and boiled. A very strong-looking ghost appeared in the middle of the water. 'Have you come to do some exercise?' she asked. 'Then catch this and start lifting.'

The ghost pulled a dumbbell from her pocket and threw it at the cat. It missed by just an inch.

'No, thanks,' said Pangur Bán. 'I'm looking for a mouse. He's grey and plump and oh-so tasty.'

'You silly cat,' the ghost replied. 'Chasing mice is not a sport. Now *climbing*, that's the thing. Last one to the climbing wall's a rotten egg!'

But Pangur Bán didn't want to climb. She was getting tired, but still she walked on alone.

Pangur Bán walked beneath a bell tower, just as the bell began to ring.

'You down there,' a voice called out. 'You silly cat. Don't you know that that's bad luck? To walk beneath the striking bell.'

'Oh, Mr Wilde,' said Pangur Bán, 'have you seen a little mouse?'

'Is he grey and plump and oh-so juicy?' said the ghost of Oscar Wilde.

'Yes!' said the cat.

'And yummy and furry and oh-so spicy?'

'Yes!' said the cat.

'And pudgy and squidgy and oh-so meaty?'

'Yes!' said the cat.

'Is he grey and plump and oh-so tasty?'

'Yes, yes!' said the cat. 'Have you seen him?'

'No, I have not,' said the ghost of Oscar Wilde. 'Now off you go, you silly cat. I've things to write – some funny plays and clever poems.'

Poor Pangur Bán walked on alone.

'Pangur Bán, there you are! I've been looking for you everywhere.'

The cat knew the friendly figure in the dark, dark night. He was the monk who had made the old, old beautiful book.

'I've been searching for a plump, grey mouse,' said Pangur Bán. 'But I can't find him anywhere!'

The friendly monk smiled.

'Come with me,' he said. 'I think I know where that plump, grey mouse will be.'

Book of Kells

Back in the library with the old, old beautiful book, the plump, grey mouse sat cleaning his ears.

'There he is!' cried Pangur Bán.

The plump, grey mouse saw the cat and gave her a very cheeky grin.

Then he turned and jumped right into the page.

Pangur Bán smiled and jumped right in behind him.

And every dark, dark night, in that very quiet library, inside that old, old beautiful book, that plump, grey mouse is still running. And Pangur Bán is still chasing him.

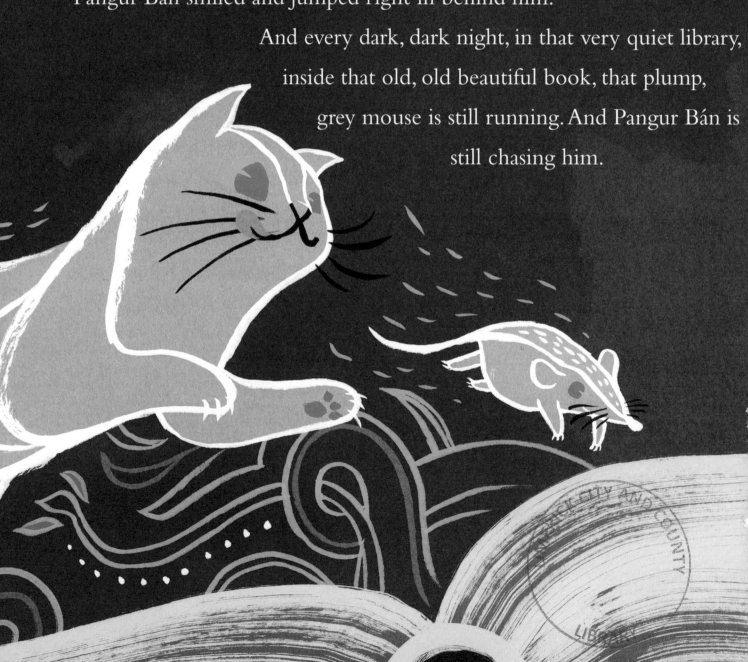

TRINITY COLLEGE GHOSTS

Jonathan Swift wrote lots of books and poems. His most famous book is *Gulliver's Travels*. Gulliver had wild adventures sailing to places like the island of Lilliput, where all the people are tiny, and the land of Brobdingnag, where all the people are giants.

Edward Ford worked in Trinity College and was very strict. One night, during a terrible argument with a group of students, he was badly injured. The students felt awful but, before he died, Edward forgave them.

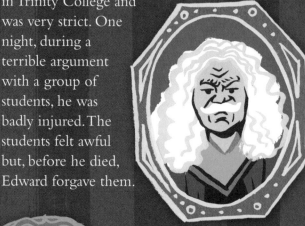

Queen Elizabeth I was the Queen of England for a very, very long time in the 1500s. Trinity College was built in Dublin while she ruled.

King Charles II was an English king who lived more than three hundred years ago. He was a benefactor who gave money to Trinity College.

Samuel Beckett wrote books, poetry and plays such as *Waiting for Godot* and *Endgame*. The theatre in Trinity College is named after him.

The Dublin University Elizabethan Society was set up in the early 1900s. Although Trinity College was one of the first big universities to let in female students, for a long time women weren't allowed to stay on campus after six o'clock, or to join any clubs. So they started their own club – 'The Eliz'.